Peter J.Marsden-Fereday is of Irish descent and has spent much of his working life as a consultant engineer with the Sheffield firm Davy's. During this time his work has taken him to places as far afield as Germany, Russia and Algeria. He was also present in Saudi Arabia after the Gulf War where he assisted in the clean-up operation following the torching of the Kuwaiti oil wells.

Describing himself as "semi-retired" he is now realising his lifelong ambition of becoming a writer, something in which he has dabbled since the age of 14. As a seasoned "Sheffielder" Peter has spent many happy years walking his beloved hills and dales in the Peak District and has been increasingly enthralled by its legends and folklore. This interest prompted him to write his first book "Peak District Poetry" (The Hallamshire Press, 1996). "Peak District Tales" is his second published work which he has written in the hope that his highly original stories will enable some of the Peaks' myths and legends to gain a new lease of life and reach a new audience for generations to come.

Overleaf: The enchanted Haddon Hall between Bakewell and Rowsley.

PEAK DISTRICT
TALES
for Young and Old

Peter J. Marsden-Fereday

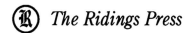 The Ridings Press

Monsal Dale – home of the wizard and the witch (Tale 9)

Photo credits: Hedgerow Publishing (Cover);
Simon Laffoley (33, 39); Duncan Smith (all other photos)
Sketches by the author

First published in 1996 by
The Ridings Press, 62 Sheldon Road, Sheffield, South Yorkshire S7 1GX

ISBN 0 9527235 1 4

Typeset by Commercial Services
Carnson House, 1 Moorgate Road, Rotherham S60 2EE
Printed and bound in Doncaster

INTRODUCTION

The Peak District National Park is not only our largest National Park but also the world's second most popular, after Mount Fuji in Japan! Like its' oriental partner, there are many legends associated with it, whose characters were once very much alive and living out the stories attributed to them. Their magical status has been defined through the fear and superstition of the surrounding ancient communities, adding a fairy tale-like quality. The following pages will introduce the reader to fairy tale castles, mermaids, giants, dwarves, dragons, witches, talking animals and flying saucers – to name but a few!

These original tales have been linked as truthfully as possible with those legendary characters, who in the past have lent so much to the folklore of the Peak District.

The author has also included a suitable moral at the end of each tale emphasizing the fact that such tales still have a place in our 'modern' society. A history file with brief directions to each location has been included at the end of each chapter for those wishing to take a magical tour of the Peak District National Park.

I hope you enjoy reading these stories as much as I enjoyed writing them, and that they encourage you to visit one of the most beautiful parts of England.

Peter J. Marsden-Fereday

MAP OF THE PEAK DISTRICT NATIONAL PARK

Numbers refer to the location of each tale
(15, 17 & 20 refer to the Peak District in general)

Contents

1. The Forgotten Castle

(Haddon Hall – 20th century)

Deserted for 200 years, Haddon Hall is visited by two local children who are invited inside by a young boy dressed in period costume, and are taken back in time.

There is in the district of Haddon, what can only be described as the most beautiful fairy castle in all England *(see frontispiece)*.

Uninhabited for some two hundred years and shrouded in mystery and legend with tales of phantoms who held watch over their past secrets, it became an ever increasing object for the curious. Such then was the temptation for which to confront its outer walls, especially by the local children.

Approaching the little bridge which crossed over the river to give access to the great castle doors, Larry and his sister Annie paused for awhile to picture the scene before them. On this very same bridge many years ago, the knights and their ladies would ride by on their way up to the great castle to take part in the lavish banquets held by the 'King of the Peak', Sir George Vernon.

Larry had often wondered what it would have been like to have lived in those chivalrous days, doing battle for King and country, jousting at the tournaments and helping the damsels in distress. Annie, on the other hand, could only think about how tired she was and suggested that it was about time they started making their way back home. Stifling a little yawn and sitting herself down on the side of the bridge, it was then that Larry reminded her of the purpose of their visit to the castle.

Having promised their friends that they would dare to run up and touch the fearsome castle doors, and knowing full well that by not doing so they would run the risk of being called names and poked fun at, Larry therefore agreed to touch the doors for both of them, much to the delight of his weary sister.

Taking a deep breath and summoning up all his courage, Larry was just about to set off when there came a strange chuckling sound from behind a nearby bush.

Springing to her feet, Annie suddenly burst out laughing at the appearance of an oddly dressed little boy, who seemingly sprang out from nowhere.

Introducing himself as Rob and admitting to having overheard their conversation, he suggested that instead of just touching the castle doors, why didn't they allow him to show them the inside of the castle as his guests.

Both Annie and Larry thought the boy to be some kind of half-wit and scoffed at the idea.

Shrugging his shoulders in seeing that they did not really quite believe him, the little boy started towards the castle alone. For a while, the two children just stared after him and then, as if reading each others thoughts, slowly they began to follow at a discreet distance.

Upon reaching the stables, which were a little way below the actual doors to the castle, Rob stopped and then turning around, asked them if they were quite sure they would not like to join him after all.

After a few minutes mumbling between themselves, Larry cautiously enquired whether there were any other people in the castle. The reply which followed stunned the children even more than when first meeting their young companion.

Rob explained, that although to those people who lived outside the castle it had indeed been deserted for some two hundred years, it was however occupied by those who had lived as long ago as four hundred years and probably many more.

"You mean ghosts?", Larry chipped in.

Ignoring Larry's untimely intervention, Rob continued to explain. "With the present owners living elsewhere, these people have become caught up in a time warp and are now exercising their rights to re-live their lives again. Under normal circumstances, yes they would most certainly have been ghosts, but can only be so now when they are returned back to their own time, and that can only happen upon the return of the rightful owners back to the castle." Excited at the prospect of entering the castle with Rob, Annie urged her brother to take up the offer. Larry however hesitated until Rob promised he would take good care of them.

Upon eventually agreeing to his sister's request, Rob then warned them that at all costs they must depart from the castle in all haste if ever the present owners were to return, solemnly pointing out that otherwise they too would be whisked back in time along with himself and his friends, never again to return to their normal lives.

Entering the stables and travelling through a secret passage which led up to and inside the castle, Rob turned to them and put his finger to his lips as he quietly nudged open a large door in front of them. The sight which followed brought gasps of amazement from both Larry and Annie.

Assembled in a great hall which confronted them were many people all wearing what appeared to be fancy-dress costumes, which Rob informed them was the dress of his period over four hundred years ago. Whilst Annie marvelled at the beautiful ladies in their ball gowns, Larry just stood and gaped, open-mouthed in disbelief.

Never had the two children imagined that behind the old castle walls such an array of grandeur and merry-making would be taking place. Acrobats cartwheeled and somersaulted across the floor while jugglers were tossing sticks of fire high into the air and then catching them with the greatest of ease. Minstrels in their gaily coloured uniforms accompanied the dancers and while all this was happening, a Jester was playfully poking fun at everyone.

So enjoyable was the occasion that hardly anyone heard the banging on the door opposite to that where the children were standing.

As the music began to fade away and each and everyone in their turn ceased whatever it was they were doing, all eyes now turned to stare in the direction of the commotion.

Without any further warning, the doors were suddenly flung wide open to reveal, broomstick in hand, the most horrible looking witch imaginable. Putting his hand to his mouth, Larry stifled a little laugh not quite believing it to be a real witch at all, not, that was, until Rob assured him that she was, and a really bad one at that.

Stepping forward from out of the crowd there appeared an elderly looking gentleman, with his long white beard waving from side to side. His bushy eyebrows were raised disapprovingly and he angrily demanded the witch to state her purpose and be gone.

Arching her back and sticking out her large pointed nose, she slowly stalked around the hall. "Ah hah!"' she cackled upon seeing Larry and Annie. "There, Sir George," she said to the elderly gentleman. "They are the purpose for my being here. I've come to take my children home," pointing her broomstick in their direction.

The children's presence, which had previously gone unnoticed in the great hall, was now quickly brought to light.

Meeting the angry gaze of his master, Rob hurriedly explained to Sir George the reason behind their intrusion.

Listening intently to Rob's story and at the same time thoughtfully stroking his long white beard, he eventually gave Rob the benefit of any doubts he might have had and believed his story to be true, at the same time ordering the witch to be seized by the guards and thrown into the dungeons.

With the festivities about to re-commence, and after Rob had been reprimanded by Sir George, there came yet another interruption, but this time far more serious than the last, with the news that the present owners had just arrived in the grounds of the castle.

The two children immediately looked to Rob for protection. Taking a firm hold of their hands, Rob swiftly ushered them back out through the doors by which they had arrived and towards the secret passage which would lead them to safety.

Running as fast as their legs would carry them, they were suddenly overtaken by a swirling rush of wind and blown right back into the great hall. All who had been present only moments ago, were now being tossed around like rag dolls, and amidst all the moaning and shrieking there then came a loud clap of thunder taking everyone back to their old lives of four hundred years ago – Larry and Annie included.

For what seemed like a lifetime being first blown one way and then another, the wind gradually came to a halt, leaving the occupants in the hall to pick themselves up and to carry on where they left off. As Larry and Annie opened their eyes, they found to their great dismay that they were now dressed as were the others befitting the period they were in.

Looking across at Rob and asking if they really had been taken back in time, he nodded sadly and confirmed their suspicions. Only Sir George offered any form of comfort by assuring them that he would do all he could to return them safely back to their own time, thus placing a silver ring on Annie's finger for safe keeping.

With the rest of Sir George's guests slowly rising to their feet, Sir George noticed how quickly his jester had recovered from the ordeal as he busily danced from one guest to another handing out masks and squeakers.

Enquiring into the nature of his antics, the excitable little man explained to Sir George that it was Halloween, the night when all spirits and ghosts may travel back and forth through time.

Tugging at his beard, Sir George then threw up his arms in jubilation, and declared that if they had all travelled back to their proper time, then surely Larry and Annie would be able to travel back to theirs. Upon hearing what Sir George had said, the two children immediately sprang to their feet asking what they could do to help, whilst Rob meanwhile had rushed off in all haste to fetch the astrologer. Where Larry and Annie's spirits had been at a low ebb, they were now full of excitement and expectation at the thought that they might be on their way home.

Feeling much more at ease, Larry and Annie were not long in joining the rest of the party in their fun and games. Musical chairs and pass the parcel were among the games they knew, but there were others which they were none too certain about, especially kiss the ghost, which they thought was very similar to postman's knock.

So wrapped up were they in the festivities that they had almost completely forgotten about their troubles.

With the arrival of Rob and the astrologer, whom the children thought looked more like a magician with his stardust cloak and pointed hat, there was then placed in the centre of the floor a large table, upon which the learned man laid out the tools of his trade.

"Halloween," he chortled. "Now let me see," he mumbled to himself as he consulted his charts of the universe.

Mixing together a few horrid looking potions and then pouring them out of one glass and into another, there then came a tiny explosion followed by a large cloud of smoke bellowing upwards, out of which, much to the delight of all present, appeared Bumpkins the dancing bear.

Dancing around the room and waving to all his friends, Bumpkins then turned to the astrologer to await his instructions. Firstly he was told that he must take Larry and Annie to meet his strange and powerful friends in the woods, who would hopefully tell them where to find the magic moonbeams which would carry them back home. Meanwhile he would consult with the stars in order to plot a safe journey home for them.

The two children, accompanied by Rob and the bear, thanked Sir George and skipped happily out of the hall to search for Bumpkin's friends. Once outside the castle, their first stop was to visit Bumpkin's oldest friend, the weeping willow tree.

Bowing gracefully and listening intently to every word of their story, the tree then began to tremble and cry non stop with tears streaming down his trunk. Feeling sorry for him, Annie asked why it was that he was crying so much.

"I'm a weeping willow," he sobbed. "I'm supposed to cry and if you had been stood in one place for years and years, then you too would weep."

Consoling his friend, Bumpkins then enquired as to the where-abouts of the magic moonbeams, at which the tree suggested they go and see the last wolf.

Furthering their journey in the direction given by the sobbing tree, it wasn't long before they came upon the hideout of the last wolf.

Having watched the group approaching his den, the wolf suddenly sprang out in front of them.

"Ger, er, er'" came the pathetic growl.

"He doesn't sound very much like a wolf," Annie declared.

"He doesn't even look much like a wolf," added Larry.

"Neither would you if you were the last wolf'" cried the animal.

Bumpkins explained that the reason why he could not make proper wolf noises, was because he had never seen another wolf and therefore didn't know how they were supposed to growl.

Again the bear related the children's story, whilst at the same time the wolf went about practising his growling.

Believing the wolf not to have heard a word he said, Bumpkins was just about to give up when the animal suddenly stopped. Looking at the children and then at the bear, he whispered secretively, "Sunny Sunflower, she will know for I believe the moonbeams rest quite close-by to where she grows. Better hurry though before she goes to sleep for the night'" he said looking up at the darkening sky and continuing to practice his growls.

Walking on a little further, Bumpkins came to a halt, and scratching his head wondered whether or not they were too late and that Sunny had gone to bed.

"Hello," came a sweet little voice.

"Sunny," yelled the bear in surprise.

Quickly he introduced his friends and then stressed how important it was that they should find the magic moonbeams.

"That's no problem," giggled Sunny. "They land close-by to where you are standing, and very soon too for that matter."

Larry and Annie could hardly contain themselves and thanked Sunny and Bumpkins with all their hearts and Rob too, who presented them with a bag full of food and sweets for their journey.

With Rob and Bumpkins moving to one side, Sunny then instructed the children exactly where to stand.

As if by magic, descending through the tree tops, the moonbeams slowly made their way down to the ground. One by one they landed, lighting up the whole forest and then, as if designed especially for Larry and Annie, two moonbeams gently slipped over them and began to raise them both off the ground.

Nervously waving their goodbyes to Sunny, Bumpkins and Rob, the two children were carefully lifted above the tree tops and in a flash were whisked off far out of sight of the onlookers. For a moment, Larry thought he could hear his sister calling his name from somewhere in the castle grounds.

Peering through the evening shadows, which had now fallen over this fairy-tale setting, Larry once again heard his name being called. "Larry, Larry, I'm falling. Help! help!" he heard Annie cry.

Running over to her side, Larry just caught hold of her before she was about to tumble off the bridge upon which she had been sitting. "Annie, Annie wake up," Larry urged his sister shaking her by the shoulders.

"Are we home yet Larry?" she asked looking around.

"Home?" queried Larry. "No, Annie, not yet, you must have been dreaming," he said, placing his arm around her.

Looking out across at the castle and then back to her brother, she sadly began to realise that she had indeed been dreaming. The weeping willow, the last wolf, Sunny and Sir George and Bumpkins, had they all been in her mind?

"But what about Rob, surely you saw Rob?", Annie pleaded.

"No, Annie, I didn't see anybody, but I did touch the castle doors for the both of us," he proudly boasted.

Slowly they made their way homeward towards the little gate which had allowed them access to the castle's grounds, Larry pleased with himself at having touched the dreaded doors, whilst Annie reflecting upon what might have been.

"If only it had been true," she thought to herself. "What a story she would have had to tell her friends."

Just as they were about to reach the entrance leading out onto the highway, they were passed by an elderly gentleman in clothing not unlike that which was worn by the local gentry.

Annie looked at him curiously as he stroked his long white beard, raised his hat and bid them good evening.

Staring in utter disbelief as she watched him make his way on towards the castle, he suddenly stopped and turned to meet Annie's gaze, giving a little bow and a wink before disappearing behind some bushes.

Instinctively Annie began to play with the ring on her finger which Sir George had given her. Smiling to herself she slowly began to recollect her thoughts about those people she had met from so very long ago.

Turning her head once again in the hope of catching just one last glimpse of the old man, she was almost certain that she saw a solitary moonbeam disappear over the fairy castle. Again she smiled.

"Sir George," she whispered, catching sight of Larry's foolish grin. "It was for real wasn't it Larry?" she asked longingly.

"Talking bears!," she heard him mutter to himself.

"Larry, Larry you were there after all," she shouted happily.

Larry threw his head back and laughed at his sister's enthusiasm, then squeezing her hand tightly he ran on ahead playfully making fun of her along the way.

THE MORAL OF THIS TALE
Dreams are what you make them.

DIRECTIONS AND HISTORY FILE

Hidden out of view on the A6 between Bakewell and Rowsley, Haddon Hall is perhaps the most romantic medieval house in all England. Built in the 12th century, Haddon was once home to the Vernon family before passing to John Manners through his well chronicled marriage to Lady Dorothy Vernon. Now in the hands of the Duke of Rutland, the Hall owes much of its well preserved appearance to the fact that it was unoccupied between the 18th and 20th centuries.

A basket of the famous Bakewell Puddings

2. The Sad Pudding and the Happy Tart

(Bakewell – 19th century)

The story of Mrs. Greaves' recipe which changed a strawberry tart into the famous Bakewell Pudding at the Rutland Hotel.

There was once upon a time an inn called the 'White Horse' which stood quite close to the market place in old Bakewell town.

Serving the needs of many a weary traveller with a bath and a bed for the night, the inn was also renowned for its good food and its mouthwatering strawberry tart, without which no self respecting traveller would ever think of leaving.

However, one day when cook was in the kitchen making the tart, a terrible thing happened.

Using the proper ingredients, she unfortunately mixed them in the wrong order and popped them in the oven to bake. Upon taking out what she thought was going to be a strawberry tart she instead took out a pudding, her mistake being that she had placed the jam in the lower half of the tart instead of on the top.

As soon as cook realised what she had done, she ran off to inform her employer, Mrs. Greaves, about the mishap.

Whilst all this was taking place and unbeknown to either cook or Mrs. Greaves, the newly baked pudding stifled a little cry. "Oh dear, oh dear, just look at me. I don't look half as pretty as I used to look."

"Ugh!" said a left-over strawberry tart. "Whatever has happened to you?".

"I know, I know," cried the bewildered pudding. "What a mess, oh what a mess I am in."

"Never mind," came the soothing reply from her friend, "Perhaps they will like you as you are."

"But I feel so crusty, and I've put on weight too," said the pudding. The left-over strawberry tart, who still looked almost as glamorous as when she had been in full bloom, cheerily tried to make light of the situation.

"They will hardly notice the difference between us they will be that hungry."

"But they will be expecting you," sobbed the pudding, "And all they will get is plain old me. Oh dear, oh dear."

At this point cook came running back into the kitchen.

"Serve it as it is, indeed" she muttered to herself quickly picking up the pudding and returning back to the dining room.

"Oh I do hope they will like pudding," purred the tart.

After a few minutes silence there was suddenly to be heard great cries of delight and shouts of "More, more," and "Seconds please." The left-over strawberry tart could hardly believe her ears, never before had she heard such compliments.

"Oh how happy I am for pudding, now we will all be liked even more than we have ever been. Wheee!" Tart stood on her edge, spun round and round and eventually fell into a pile of crumbs upon the floor.

THE MORAL OF THIS TALE
Eat with your mouth and not with your eyes.

DIRECTIONS AND HISTORY FILE

The only remaining part of the 'White Horse' hostelry has now been blended into the 'Rutland Arms" in Bakewell town centre, and can be seen on the corner of the A6 and the B5055 leading to Monyash.

The famous Bakewell Pudding may be purchased at various 'pudding shops' within the market town. However, all visitors should be warned never to call it a 'tart' as the locals remain ever proud of their tradition, even if it once was a strawberry tart before Mrs. Greaves decided the mistake was 'genuine'.

3. The Doctor's Gate

(Longdendale – 17th century)

A local magician, nicknamed Dr. Faust after the famous German sorcerer, challenges the Devil to a race down an old Roman road.

If ever there was any magic to be found in the hills and dales of the Peak District, then it would most surely be found in Longdendale.

Long ago when King Arthur ruled at Camelot, Merlin, his chief advisor and the most powerful wizard on earth, is reputed to have actually passed through this dark and mysterious valley, and by tradition the spells he left behind are still practised by the people who live there.

A local magician who was nicknamed 'Doctor Faust' after the great German sorcerer, was above all the finest wizard in this valley. So good was he that one day he set about to prove just how strong his powers really were, by challenging the very devil himself to see who was the greatest sorcerer of all, both from this world and the devil's own.

Upon hearing of the doctor's rash challenge, the devil speedily made his way to Longdendale in order not only to accept the challenge, but also to defeat the doctor on his own ground and thus claim his mortal soul.

Agreeing the terms laid down by each other, they decided upon a race down the old Roman road which passes close by the doctors little village of Mossy Lee, extending to the Roman fort at Brough.

With the arrival of the day of the race, the entire population of Longdendale turned out to witness the doctor's amazing challenge. Witches and magicians with their apprentices, sorcerers, gypsies and travelling people and even the witches cats, all appeared as if out of nowhere.

As the two contestants lined up at the start a great cheer went up and at the drop of a witches hat, they were off.

To the disappointment of the locals, the devil soon took an early lead and was well clear of the doctor, who for some unknown reason appeared to be in no hurry at all.

With his supporters yelling and cheering him on to go faster, the doctor still kept up his steady pace and it wasn't long before the devil was well out of sight.

Turning to look over his shoulder, the devil smiled wickedly to himself at the idea of the foolish magician ever thinking that he could outsmart the master of wizardry. The doctor meanwhile plodded on seemingly without a care in the world, and with a smile upon his face, for further along the road he could just make out the form of the devil, huffing and puffing and shouting and cursing as he came to a halt by a tiny trickling stream.

Drawing up alongside his opponent, the doctor gave a sly sideways grin, crossed the stream and went on to win handsomely.

The celebrations which followed that night in Longdendale were long remembered for how the doctor tricked the devil at his own game. For the few outsiders who had watched the race out of sheer curiosity, it was explained why and how the doctor knew he would eventually win.

To those who study the mysterious arts of the unexplained, it is common knowledge that members of the spirit world cannot cross over water. The doctor, having done his homework, knew well of the land and its stream by living close to the old road and had no fear as to the outcome. On the other hand, the devil had been so obsessed with gaining the doctor's soul, he had realised too late that he had been outwitted. The area is still known as the 'Doctor's Gate'.

THE MORAL OF THIS TALE
Do not cross your bridges before you come to them.

DIRECTIONS AND HISTORY FILE

The 'Doctor's Gate' lies off the A57 Snake Pass, four miles east of Glossop and can only be approached on foot. The name of the local sorcerer is not quite certain, but he was known to have had powers far beyond the norm.

19

4. The Mermaid Queen

(Kinder Scout – 20th century)

A tale about two friends who decide to seek out the mermaid who reputedly sits by this pool granting everlasting life to those who catch sight of her.

High up on Kinder Scout there is a stretch of water known as the 'Mermaid's Pool' due to the many reports made by people claiming to have seen a water spirit there in the form of a mermaid. This lifeless pool is also believed to be connected with the distant Atlantic Ocean because of its salty water, whereby no animal will be seen to drink from it and no fish has been known to survive its murky depths.

According to legend, anyone sighting the mermaid at one minute past the hour of midnight on Easter eve, would either receive the gift of eternal life or else be dragged down under the water to their death.

Young Lennie Robinson and his friend Barry Butler decided one Easter holiday to set up camp on the mountain in the hope of catching a glimpse of the mermaid.

Filled with thoughts of everlasting life, they jokingly made their way up the difficult slopes wondering whether or not they would remain at their youthful twelve years of age, if of course they actually met up with the mermaid.

Reaching the mermaid's pool, the mists were now all around them as is usually the case on Kinder Scout. Slowly they began to unpack and pitch their tent, checking their watches in the process and at the same time keeping an anxious eye on the mysterious pool.

Trying desperately to keep awake, the two boys having had their supper then decided to go for a stroll around the now moonlit and eerie water's edge.

Lennie, sandwich in hand, walked silently by the pool, kicking at the occasional pebble whilst Barry began to skim stones across the flat watery surface. Bending down to pick up another stone, it was then that Barry thought he caught sight of something in the centre of the pool.

Yelling out to Lennie and running over to where he was stood, Barry swore on oath that he had definitely seen something move. Then just as Lennie was about to scold his friend, there came a resounding splash close by to where they were standing.

Turning their heads towards the disturbance, they were just in time to see a large fishy tail disappearing back into the water. The two chums could hardly believe their eyes and before they could pass comment on the matter, up popped the mermaid right beside them.

"Hello," she said, startling the boys by her sudden appearance. "Well I must say," she went on, combing her dripping hair. "What a fine looking couple of young gentlemen you are."

"Are you the m-m-m-mermaid?" stammered Barry.

"Of course she's a mermaid," said Lennie.

"How do you do," Barry politely enquired.

"How do I do? How do I do what?" giggled the mermaid.

Lennie began to study the image before them. She was neither young nor was she old, she was undoubtedly very beautiful he thought, but perhaps a little dim.

"What Barry meant is, hello and how are you?", Lennie started to explain.

"How am I what?" she answered, slightly annoyed and smacking her tail down hard upon the marshy floor. "I am a mermaid, surely you must have noticed that. My goodness, what a silly question!".

"Would you like a sandwich?" Barry offered.

"I only eat sea food thank you very much," she retorted, now showing signs of distress.

"Sorry," Barry apologised, "I only thought you might be hungry with there not being any fish in the pool."

"That's what you think," she said leaning closer to the two boys. "Can you keep a secret?" she asked them.

"Oh yes, yes," replied both Lennie and Barry.

"Well then, come a little closer and I will tell you all about what lies at the bottom of my pool."

At this they warily moved themselves nearer to the mermaid, and Barry being the closest, felt his hand being taken by that of the mysterious creature as she flopped up to him.

"Now," continued the mermaid. "Where I come from there is a secret which no humans have ever known and the only way for you to find out, is for both of you to come with me and to see it with your own eyes."

"No, no," shouted Lennie backing away. "Let go of her hand Barry, come on, come on." But as much as Barry tried to heed his friends warning, he remained firmly fixed in the mermaid's grip, and before Lennie could assist his friend further, there followed a sudden movement by the mermaid then a terrific splash. Both the mermaid and Barry disappeared below the murky surface of the water.

"Barry, Barry," cried Lennie in vain. Lennie just stood there staring at the now still water, hardly able to believe his eyes.

Beneath the water, the mermaid swam deeper and deeper, still keeping a firm hold on Barry's hand. Meanwhile, Barry could not understand why he was still able to breathe having been underwater for so long without air.

It seemed that the further they went, the deeper they went and then just as Barry thought that he would never again see the light of day, there appeared in front of them a brilliant glow seemingly leading to the surface.

With the rushing of water in his ears, the mermaid gave Barry one gigantic shove and before he knew what was happening, he found himself sitting in a wonderland beyond his wildest dreams.

Everything around him was like that of a large painting but with all the colours apparently in the wrong places. The sky was a pale yellow with a crimson sun, the trees although their leaves were green all had purple trunks and on the shore where they had landed, the sand was a mixture of gold and silver stardust. Sitting on the softly shaded grass around him, were animals and people all appearing to talk to one another at the same time, with enough food, fruits and drinks to last a lifetime.

The mermaid, having now slipped out of the water to sit by Barry's side, explained how everyone and every beast had been granted the gift of eternal life, and that if he so desired the same gift would be bestowed upon him.

Taking in the scene before him, Barry thought how nice it would be not to have to go to school any more; no more homework, no more rain and no more having to get up early in the morning, but most of all, he thought with a smile, no more cabbage!

Before he could ask the mermaid any questions, she once again inquired whether or not he would like to stay and live a life everlasting. Barry's reply was that although it would be very nice to live forever, it would also be very lonely because all his friends lived in the real world where he was quite happy to remain.

The mermaid upon hearing this was furious, smacking her tail repeatedly up and down on the sand.

"Do you or don't you?" she demanded.

Barry was very tempted indeed and wondered what Lennie would do. "Lennie, Lennie," he shouted. "I almost forgot." He then stood up, turned to the mermaid and pleaded with her to take him back as Lennie would be wondering what had happened to him.

"You cannot have eternal life on your earth, only down here may you have that," she scoffed.

Barry looked at the mermaid and told her that if such was the case, then all who lived in her world were in actual fact not alive but dead.

"Precisely," she mocked, throwing her head back scornfully.

"Then all I can say," replied Barry, "Is that I would rather be alive in my world than dead in yours." Immediately he had uttered the words he found himself once again in the water being dragged along at great speed.

"Barry, Barry," he heard Lennie calling. "Barry where are you?".

Barry suddenly found himself staring out across the magic pool, not quite believing what had happened to him and wondering if anything ever had, since his clothes were still dry.

"There you are," came Lennie's voice. "I've been looking all over the place for you, where have you been?".

"I . . I . . I," Barry stammered.

"I've packed the tent up and I think we'd better go home since nothing's going to happen up here and in any case, it's well past the hour of midnight now," Lennie said with a big yawn.

Still in a daze, Barry wondered why Lennie remained unaware of his absence and the more he thought about it, the more inclined he was to believe that it might after all have just been a dream.

"Come on," shouted Lennie, making his way down the darkened slope. The two boys walked along in silence. Lennie thinking to himself that he must have been stupid to have ever dreamed of undertaking such a venture, whilst Barry thought thoughts to the contrary, dream or no dream.

Carefully picking their way across the marshes and disturbing the occasional rabbit with their torchlight, Lennie muttered "Mermaids, ugh!" as if in disbelief.

"It's just a fairy tale isn't it Lennie?" Barry queried searchingly.

"Aye, just a fairy tale Barry," came the disgruntled reply.

Allowing a little smile to cross his face, Barry took out his gloves from his pocket and pulled them on over his hands, but had he looked behind him at that instance he would have noticed a tiny sprinkling of stardust falling from his pocket.

THE MORAL OF THIS TALE
Some thoughts are best kept to yourself.

DIRECTIONS AND HISTORY FILE

The Mermaid's Pool, which lies close to Kinder Downfall high up on Kinder Scout, may only be reached via the Pennine Way either from Hayfield on the A624 or the Snake Pass A57. It is advisable, if not knowing this area, to only attempt this climb in the company of experienced walkers.

Lennie and Barry with the mermaid on Kinder Scout.

5. Fairy Land

(Deep Dale – 18th century)

> The adventures of two sisters who dare to enter the land of the fairies.

The reason why fairies are usually only seen by children, is that they have very little time to listen to the silly talk of grown-ups, who are forever claiming that they do not exist. Another reason could well be that grown-ups are much larger than children, making it all the more difficult when stealing them to take back to fairy land.

The fairies of Deep Dale are well known throughout the Peak District from their many sightings, and are believed to have made their home within the grassy slopes and rocky tors which descend to the shadowy depths of the valley. In all there are reputed to be up to nine hundred of these little creatures dwelling in Deep Dale, hence its popular name of 'Fairy Land'.

Young Jenny Smith and her sister Rose were no strangers to the ways of the fairies, and would often go to meet them and listen to their tales. They always took the usual precautions: never to wear the colour green, this being the fairies favourite colour at which they would take offence should anyone be seen wearing it; and never ever to visit them on a Friday, for this was the day when the fairy Queen held her court and no humans were allowed to see them.

Jenny and Rose, although having been accepted by the fairies, had never been invited into their domain and were treated with a little caution due to their gypsy background. However, being children of the earth, like the fairies, they were held in some respect in sharing the same powers which ordinary people did not possess. Soon all this was to change!

Having celebrated Halloween with the local children, Jenny and Rose decided to take a short cut through Deep Dale back to their parents caravan. Well aware of the dangers of meeting the little folk on this, one of the special nights, they nevertheless danced and frolicked along at a leisurely pace still full of high spirits and still wearing their masks.

Upon reaching the place where they knew the fairies to be, they then foolishly dared one another to attract the fairies attention by dancing around the grassy mounds. They hoped to trick the fairies by hiding their identity behind their masks in order to see fairy land. Holding hands and dancing in a circle, slowly they began to count out the magic number of rings required.

"One, two, three, four, five, six, seven, eight," and then with one almighty shout, "NINE!"

What happened next was to stop the two children instantly in their tracks. Beneath the ground where they stood came a great rumbling sound, followed by a large cavern opening up before them. Nervously peering inside, they were then confronted by a tiny little elf who invited them to enter.

Rose carefully studied the elf and remembered the many stories she had heard about how they would steal children away from their parents, then put them to work serving their greedy needs. Hesitant as she was, her sister Jenny took hold of her hand and before she could decide upon the best course of action, found herself being led through the dark passageway.

For what seemed like an eternity, the two sisters and the elf, walked, stumbled and crawled along the wet and uneven tunnel. Eventually turning a corner and passing through a secret doorway, they reached the land of the fairies.

Under a dazzling array of colourful twinkling lights, the fairy folk were all busy making merry. Soft music filled the huge grotto which appeared to be endless, banquets were being held with wondrous sweetmeats to choose from, with dancing taking place just about everywhere, and for those who wished to rest, sumptuous couches awaited their tired little bodies.

Jenny and Rose could hardly believe their eyes at the scene set before them. Everything a child could possibly wish for was provided. So tempting were the niceties offered that Jenny would have taken part in the fun and games had not her sister held her back. Rose, who was the younger of the two, was not particularly any wiser than her sister, but being the youngest she was able to remember more vividly the fairy tales told them by their mother.

It is common belief among country folk, that if upon accepting the fairies hospitality and by drinking and eating and joining in their festivities, you will automatically be imprisoned in fairy land for the rest of your life. Although Jenny had forgotten most of the old tales, Rose remembered in horror when their mother used to pretend to be the Fairy Queen and chase them around their beds. She reminded Jenny of this, much to her bitter disappointment.

After refusing the fairies tempting offers, the sisters then took off their halloween masks and upon being recognised, were immediately presented with a string of beads apiece as a token of the fairies friendship to remind them of their visit.

Placing the beads around their necks and being told that their allotted time in fairy land was at an end, they were then escorted back to where they had first entered.

Having returned back to the safety of the normal world, the two sisters hugged each other happily and laughed at the thought of having deceived the fairies, but their laughter was to be short lived.

Looking down at the beautiful beads around her neck, Jenny suddenly let out a terrible scream, ripping them off and throwing them to the ground with Rose doing likewise, for all they saw was a string of weeds covered with creepy crawlies!

THE MORAL OF THIS TALE
All that glistens is not gold.

DIRECTIONS AND HISTORY FILE

Deep Dale lies three miles east of Buxton on the A6 and can be reached by travelling through King Sterndale. Myths of giants and hobs are commonplace here, dating as far back as prehistoric times.
Legend has it that within the realms of Deep Dale when the valley is lit by the moon, nocturnal festivities are said to take place, especially among the fairies.

Rose leading Jenny on their way into fairy land.

6. The Bakewell Witches

(Bakewell – 1608)

The story of the mistaken identity of Mrs. Stafford and her sister who were accused of being witches after letting out a room in their millinery shop.

Market day in the town of Bakewell is always full of interesting things to see and do, with people scampering around trying to secure the best buys, market traders shouting out their wares and farmers who have brought their livestock to sell and exchange in the cattle market. Apart from these honest working folk, there are of course always those who seek to profit from those good people by dishonest means: thieves, pickpockets, poachers and tricksters to name a few, who upon their hour of treachery then appear to vanish into thin air.

Living quite closeby to the market place was a very respectable lady by the name of Mrs. Stafford, who, along with her sister, made hats and gowns in their little shop which they would then sell to the public. Having ample accommodation for their stock, they decided to rent out an upstairs room which had been empty for much too long and at the same time bring in a little well needed extra income.

One evening when the market had closed and the weary travellers were either making their way home or seeking refreshment at the local inn, there came a Scotsman knocking at the door of Mrs. Stafford's sewing shop, enquiring after bed and board for the night.

Letting the man in and showing him the spare room upstairs, the Scotsman immediately agreed to the terms and promised to settle his bill the following morning.

Just as the Scotsman was about to retire in his newly acquired room, he could not help but notice a small crack in the floor. Further inspection revealed a view of Mrs. Stafford's sewing room, with numerous hats and gowns of various shapes and sizes all neatly arranged for the following day's business.

The Scotsman smiled to himself with the thought that the long flowing cloaks and funny hats could well have belonged to a couple of witches. Slowly he returned to his bed, blew out the candle and in no time at all was fast asleep.

Early the next morning, Mrs. Stafford entered the Scotsmans room with a pot of tea and a basin of hot water for him to wash himself, and at the same time asking for the nights rent.

Relying upon Mrs. Stafford's charity and good nature, the Scotsman reluctantly owned up to not having a penny piece to his name, whereby she then gathered his clothes together with the promise of returning them to him on payment of the rent owed to her.

Leaving the shop and out on to the street with only his under clothes to cover his half naked body, the Scotsman then devised a plan by which to get his own back.

After walking several miles on the open road to London and being well aware of his scant appearance, he knew that it would not be long before he was arrested and taken to a court of law to explain his lack of clothing, which was precisely what happened.

Appearing in front of the magistrate, the Scotsman began to unveil his web of deceit. Firstly he told how, when renting a room for the night at Mrs. Stafford's shop, he had heard the owner and her sister chanting and baying to the moon, and after enquiring as to what they were doing, how they had cast a spell upon him whereby he was whisked high and away over the chimney tops. All this and still dressed in his night clothes and if proof be needed, the court would surely find his daily clothes back at the shop in the town of Bakewell.

Although the Scotman's story sounded rather far-fetched, it was however a period of English history when witch-hunts were considered more a sport than an administration of the law.

Giving the Scotsman the benefit of the doubt, and after wrongly believing his story to be true by the presence of his clothing, Mrs. Stafford and her sister were found guilty of witchcraft and executed accordingly.

THE MORAL OF THIS TALE
Do not believe all you see.

DIRECTIONS AND HISTORY FILE

The market town of Bakewell is to be found on the A6 between Ashford-in-the-Water and Rowsley.

7. The Dwarf of Ashford

(Ashford-in-the-Water – 1722-1811)

> The story of Molly Bray, the Ashford beggar.

Many years ago there was to be found sat beside the old Ashford road, a poor unfortunate by the name of Molly Bray. No taller than three feet in height, she would tuck her legs beneath her cloak, put on her best smile and rely upon the generosity shown by the wealthy travellers to throw her a few coppers from passing stage coaches.

Although she was not really classed a beggar, there were some folk in the village who did not entirely agree with what she did and for those foolish enough to speak their minds, they often as not met with unexplained ill luck.

With her knobbly stick and smoking pipe she could most certainly have been mistaken for a witch, and had it not been for her Christian up-bringing, would most certainly have been deemed to be so.

Late one afternoon when making her way home from her daily routine, Molly happened to notice one of her neighbours kissing and flirting on the open highway with old soldier John who lived closeby, this particular neighbour being one of the ringleaders in tarnishing her good name. Now in these days of strict religious practices and god-fearing people, it was thought to be very undignified for a lady to be in the company of a man friend without a chaperone, and this to Molly was a chance to get some of her own back.

Knowing full well that her neighbour would not want a scandal and also that she thought Molly a witch, Molly then began to devise a plan which would perhaps silence her talkative neighbour once and for all.

On approaching the couple, she insisted that they both be married straightaway due to having been caught in such immoral circumstances, and that she would perform the ceremony herself on her broomstick over the tops of the houses.

So afraid were they that Molly would indeed carry out her intentions, they fled as fast as they could in order to be wed without any further delay, and were never seen in the village again.

Little Molly Bray had lived in Ashford for as long as anyone could remember, even the children who had grown into adults would remark upon how she had barely changed throughout the years, surviving generation after generation.

Having been a somewhat permanent fixture sitting by the wayside for all those years, there came one morning when the villagers were mystified as to Molly's whereabouts when her presence was no more.

Checking her cottage and the surrounding hillsides to no avail, the disappearance of Molly Bray became an ever increasing topic of conversation. Some said that she flew away on her broomstick, whilst others would believe that she had made enough money to retire to a place where she would be free from interfering busybodies, thus living the respectable and righteous life she so desperately sought.

THE MORAL OF THIS TALE
Judge not by appearances.

DIRECTIONS AND HISTORY FILE

The picturesque village of Ashford-in-the-Water nestles one and a half miles north west of Bakewell on the A6.
One of the many interesting features about this village is the packhorse bridge spanning the River Wye, along with its adjacent stone sheep dip which attracts many a curious visitor.

The sheep-wash bridge at Ashford-in-the-Water.

8. The Giant of Hathersage

(Hathersage – 12th century)

> How Little John grew up to become the friend and Lieutenant of Robin Hood

Long long ago in the sleepy little village of Hathersage, there lived in a hillside cottage a boy of great height and enormous strength. So huge was he that he became quite afraid of his powerful ability and would rather walk away from trouble than face it.

Known locally as the gentle giant and towering head and shoulders above all the other boys of his own age, he was therefore often called names and made fun of. One such name was, 'Little John, the Nailor's son'.

John Little, for that was his rightful name, would rise early each morning, fetch and chop the wood for the fire then race across the fields to collect food from the nearby farm for his mother – and if this wasn't enough, he would then help his father making and selling nails by which to earn their living.

Poor as they were, young John never asked for more than that which he knew his parents could afford, but like all children his age it did not stop him dreaming. His thoughts were always that perhaps one day he would make enough money to be able to buy his own farm, instead of having to work so hard for the poor returns his parents received.

As the years went by John grew taller and taller, until it wasn't long before he soon became known and recognised throughout the entire Hope Valley. Not that this worried him unduly, but it was a time when all the fit and able your men were being taken away to fight for the evil Prince John who, in the absence of his brother King Richard, had seized the throne of England for himself.

Realising the hardship which his absence would incur upon his parents, John therefore decided to go to Nottingham to sort out the matter with the sheriff.

Travelling through the Peak District, which during this time bordered on the notorious Sherwood Forest, he recalled the stories his father had told him of the dangers of the forest, namely thieves, vagabonds and murderers. John however, being frightened of no man, strode boldly forward in search of his goal.

Although the birds and the animals were friendly towards him, he still kept a sharp lookout for anyone who might try to relieve him of his purse, and as if confirming his suspicions he did not have to wait long. The story describing the first meeting between Little John and Robin Hood is legendary, and after their brief exchange of blows in the greenwood, they were to become life long friends.

When Robin first heard about Little John's intentions to seek out the sheriff of Nottingham with his troubles, the outlaw took John to one side and introduced him to the many other poor unfortunates who also had sought fair justice from that quarter.

Beneath the glades in this vast forest, Little John saw hundreds of people both young and old alike. The story was a familiar one to John. Rather than remaining in their own homes and being subjected to the unjust laws of Prince John, they had decided to live under the protection of Robin Hood and fight the evil Prince until their rightful King, Richard the 1st, returned to England.

It did not take Little John long to realise where his loyalties lay. By helping the men of Sherwood in what was to be a long and bitter struggle, his beliefs were eventually rewarded with the return of the rights of free men and the homecoming of his King, Richard the Lionheart of England.

THE MORAL OF THIS TALE
Have faith in your beliefs.

DIRECTIONS AND HISTORY FILE

On the A625 between Fox House and Bamford, Little John's grave will be found in the churchyard of St. Michaels in Hathersage. The grave is some fourteen feet in length and is set between two Yew trees. Other points of interest in the church include the 'Eyre' family brasses from which rubbings may be taken.

Little John's grave at Hathersage.

9. The Wizard and the Witch

(Monsal Dale – 19th century)

The story of Neddy Higgins and his daughter Betty who lived in a cave casting spells and making prophecies for the good of the community. Some said they were evil fairies.

Divided by the river Wye, Monsal Dale is one of the most breathtaking views in the whole of the Peak District *(see page 4)* . It is also renowned as being one of the many haunts frequented by the fairy folk and other legendary characters.

Living in a recess among the many rocks which abound in this valley, Neddy Higgins and his daughter Betty were looked upon by the local community as not only being strange but perhaps belonging to the very devil himself, or even the fairies for that matter.

Although appearing pleasant enough, they were nevertheless treated with a certain amount of mistrust due to their unkempt appearance and were often referred to as the 'Wizard and the Witch'.

One day in the nearby village of Little Longstone, there was a great commotion over the misplacement of some sheep. The villagers having searched high and low for the missing animals without success, eventually turned their attentions towards the old man and his daughter. Armed with pitchforks and heavy sticks the unruly crowd set forth to where the recess opened out in the rocky hillside, calling upon the couple to show their faces.

With all the commotion taking place outside his humble retreat, it was not long before Neddy appeared in the little opening to politely enquire as to the nature of their business.

The crowd immediately shrank back as he looked them over, but there was one who demanded to know whether or not he or his daughter had taken any sheep which did not belong to them.

Asking his would-be accusers where they had last seen the missing sheep, and after a few wild directions, he then pointed towards a bend in the river where the grass was plentiful and also where there would be ample shelter in the case of bad weather.

With looks of disbelief, the crowd reluctantly dispersed to slowly make their way to the spot so mentioned by the old man.

Spreading out on both sides of the river they began to search all the likely places where the elusive sheep might have wandered. It was not until finally reaching the location which had previously been mentioned by Neddy, that a great cry went up and to the amazement of all, there grazing in the long grass were the missing sheep.

The predictions of Neddy Higgins and his daughter soon spread to other regions of the Peak District, and it was not long before people from all walks of life began to bring their problems to the odd couple, for which they hardly ever failed to give a reasonable and truthful solution.

Although it is common belief that wizards and witches are supposed to be bad, Neddy and Betty Higgins proved over and over again to the contrary. Even during one long summer's drought when the local crops suffered due to the lack of rain, it was said that they were able to produce rain clouds for a full five days. Thus saving the crops and enabling the villagers to store enough water for the rest of the year.

For all their kindly deeds it must be noted that Neddy and his daughter never once asked for anything in return from their neighbours, as they willingly gave aid to anyone who sought their advice. However, there were those who believed them to belong to the fairy folk, pouring scorn upon them and insisting they be driven away or even burned at the stake as witches.

It was hardly surprising therefore that with the many rumours being circulated as to the origin of Neddy and his daughter, one day the villagers found them no longer in the vicinity of Monsal Dale.

THE MORAL OF THIS TALE
Do unto others as you would have them do unto yourself.

DIRECTIONS AND HISTORY FILE

Monsal Head overlooks Monsal Dale and stands by the side of the B6465 at Little Longstone between Wardlow and Ashford-in-the-Water. Famous for its viaduct over the river Wye, Monsal Dale is reputed to be one of the most haunted places in the Peak District.

10. Daft Sammy

(Castleton – 1806-1868)

> The rise of young Samuel Eyre from working in the lead mines to becoming Castleton's first unofficial tourist guide.

Young Sammy Eyre had worked in the lead mines high above Castleton for as long as he dared remember, and whilst hating every minute of it, often would he dream of the day when he no longer had to work in such appalling conditions.

Each morning he would be at the mine at six o'clock sharp and would rarely return home before ten in the evening.

For a boy of only eight years of age it was common practice to be sent to work in the mines to earn their keep, usually spending the rest of their lives in this gruesome trade and dying quite young. Sammy, however, had other ideas. Not for him were the long hours working underground in floods and falls, slithering and sliding in the slimy tunnels and never seeing the light of day.

Sammy spent what precious little time he had left to himself in his beloved Castleton running after the visiting stage coaches to offer his services to the passengers, with the hope of showing them around the beautiful countryside of which he was so proud.

Known locally as 'Daft Sammy', for his enthusiasm in earning a few extra coppers from the sightseers, his nickname brought howls of delight from the locals.

"Look yon, there runs 'Daft Sammy'. Must be visitors in Castleton" they would say. But not so daft was Sammy, for he had come to know all the many interesting places in his village and the day trippers would listen to his every word.

He would tell them tales about the lad and lass who were brutally slain on the Winnats Pass when eloping to the Peak forest, set upon by some drunken lead-miners who then met their own deaths, some say by the ghosts of the murdered couple.

Then he would go on to mention Mam Tor, with its Iron Age fort, known also as the shivering mountain due to its many landslides. Among his many other stories, Sammy told of the Norman knights of Peveril and of the illegitimate son of William the Conqueror who was to build the fairytale Peveril castle which overlooks Castleton *(see front cover)*. Furthermore he would then take his visitors to the Peak Cavern which once housed a village of rope-makers, shops and a tavern, but above all these many splendid sights there was none so more captivating than Castleton's famous 'Blue John' stone, which cannot be found anywhere else except in Sammy's village.

By helping the ladies down from their coaches and over the streams, Sammy would then be rewarded by their gentlemen friends in return for which he related his stories.

Saving a little money from what he earned by working in the mines, along with the tips he made in his spare time, Sammy was soon able to leave his regular job to be duly elected the unofficial guide of Castleton.

THE MORAL OF THIS TALE
Look after your coppers and they will look after you.

DIRECTIONS AND HISTORY FILE

Castleton is the last village in the Hope valley west of the A625. Renowned for its many dazzling show caverns, this 'Jewel of the Peak' not only has boat trips on underground canals, but also high elevations with easy access in order to view entirely both the Hope and the Edale valleys.

Daft Sammy welcoming a coachload of visitors to Castleton.

37

11. The Nine Ladies

(Stanton Moor – 18th century)

> A fertility dance where all were turned to stone.

High above the tiny village of 'Stanton in the Peak', there is a wild and lonely moor where there are many stone circles reputedly said to have been built by the ancient Druids. Common belief is that they were erected for the purpose of human sacrifice, and that their stone possesses certain magical qualities still sought after by practising witches in the area. However, there is one such circle which is not attributed to that ancient race, but of a more recent and Christian origin.

Stanton Moor has long held a temptation for the children in the outlying villages to climb these mysterious heights, meeting with their friends and indulging in the fun and games offered by this wild terrain.

Late one Saturday night it is said that nine maidens accompanied by a fiddler climbed up onto the moor to perform a fertility dance, which, according to folklore, would enhance their dreams of acquiring a husband. Forming a circle in true tradition and holding hands, at the fiddler's command they then commenced to dance round and around atop the heathered moor. So happy and carefree were they with thoughts of wedded bliss as the fiddler's tune weaved its magic spell to fever pitch, that they lost all track of time and before they knew it a distant church clock began to strike out the hour of midnight.

It was upon the twelfth chime of the clock that a strange occurrence took place on this dark and desolate moor. As if struck by lightening and before the nine maidens could take another step or the fiddler play another note, all were instantly turned to stone.

Presumably having danced into the morning of the sabbath, a sin which at that time was deemed ungodly and is still frowned upon by some communities, it was considered just desert that such a punishment should befit the crime as a warning to all other maidens when visiting Stanton Moor.

The unpleasant reminder of this misdemeanour, namely 'The Nine Ladies' stone circle, may still be seen along with the 'King (fiddler's) Stone' situated a short distance away.

THE MORAL OF THIS TALE
Life is what you make it.

DIRECTIONS AND HISTORY FILE

Turn off the A6 at Rowsley and take the B5056 to the village of Stanton in the Peak where the 'Nine Ladies Stone Circle' is sign-posted for access by bridlepath only.
At one time the 'Nine Ladies' were encompassed by a stone wall, fortunately this has since been removed allowing it to blend naturally into the setting of the more ancient circles.

The magical Nine Ladies Stone Circle at Stanton-in-the Peak.

12. Prince Arthur's Wish

(Haddon Hall – 1501)

The Crown Prince of England who wished for a bride only to repay the favour with his life.

There is a particularly serene beauty about the River Wye which is not shared by other rivers in the Peak District. Silent, easy flowing and seemingly going nowhere, it was perhaps with this in mind that the Crown Prince of England decided to stroll by these waters one pleasant autumnal evening.

The young Prince Arthur was known to have spent many blissful, and at times lonely, periods with his governor Sir Henry Vernon at nearby Haddon Hall.

Although outwardly he portrayed a gentle and sweet tempered youth, his innermost thoughts were racked with the possibility of spending the rest of his life without the courtly attributes of a bride. Albeit enjoying the balls and the banquets which had been prepared especially for his visit to Haddon Hall, the Crown Prince nevertheless tired of such frivolities and wished only for the comfort and solitude offered by his walks along the river.

It was on one of these excursions that he came to rest by an old Saxon cross just south of Hassop at Four Lane Ends, sitting himself down on the grassy bank to reflect upon his future.

With the shades of the autumn evening spreading swiftly over this tranquil setting, the young Prince sighed heavily and wished his soul for a darling wife. Resting his head between his knees it was not long thereafter that he fell into a deep sleep.

Four Lane Ends is well known throughout the Peak District as the haunt of spectres and ghouls where one might encounter a member of that darksome world. Whilst Arthur was asleep at the foot of the cross, a strange vision came to him in the form of a lady dressed all in white.

The following is a description of her, often referred to whenever relating this tale.

" . . . her features were sunken and wan, her lips of an ashy hue, and her eye-balls protruding, bright, and motionless. Pointing her fleshless finger towards his face, she spoke as follows."

"Unhappy royal Prince, mourn not that fate which is not thine! One earthly pageant awaits thee, yes, it is at hand; and then, ah! then, thou wilt drop into the lap of thy mother – thy mother earth! forth comes to Britain's shore thy lovely, smiling bride – ah! ah! bride and widow of a royal boy!"

Unbeknown at the time to Prince Arthur, there had been arranged by his selfish father, King Henry VII of England, a betrothal of marriage to Catherine of Aragon, the daughter of the Spanish King Ferdinand, when Arthur was only twelve years old.

Awakening from his dream, the Prince despondently made his way back towards Haddon trying to piece together what fragments of the vision he could remember.

Slowly he began to recall what the lady in white had told him, realising that he may not after all have to spend the rest of his life alone. Gradually increasing his pace, and still in wonderment at what the vision meant exactly, he was greeted upon his return to the Hall with the most astonishing news.

That very day his Spanish bride-to-be had landed in England and he was to be married without further delay.

As he was heir to the throne of England, he now also realised that he too could have an heir to follow in his footsteps. It was a joyous moment indeed as the prophesy of the vision had seemingly come true – that was until after only being wed four short months, the rest of the vision came to light.

The young Prince succumbed to illness and to everyones amazement died just as the vision had foretold, his last words being - - - "O, the vision of the cross at Haddon!"

There is a dreadful irony to this tale however emerging from Prince Arthur's traumatic quest to secure himself a bride. Whereupon finding the happiness which had for so long eluded him, and departing from this life at such a tender age, he left behind not only the crown of England, which would have been rightfully his, but also the hand in marriage of his widow, Catherine of Aragon, to his younger brother Henry VIII who was to wed no less than six times in all!

For almost twenty years Catherine remained faithful to Henry, and although several children were born, only the Princess Mary was to live past infancy – a good enough reason, or so Henry thought, to cause him to seek womanly attentions elsewhere in order to bear him the son he so desperately yearned for.

That the death of Henry's sons was just retribution for him marrying his brother's widow, was perhaps a convenient pretence on his part to spread his wings – or did it really go further than that? Perhaps all the way back to the cross at Haddon?

THE MORAL OF THIS TALE

To have nothing one must first give up everything.

DIRECTIONS AND HISTORY FILE

Central to the medieval Haddon Hall on the A6 and the tiny village of Hassop through which passes the B6001, are the cross-roads where the crown Prince Arthur would often toy with his thoughts. When upon returning to London, the Prince would often refer to *'Peakrell'* as that wild and wasted land, but not without a certain amount of charm.

Prince Arthur sees a ghostly vision at Four Lane Ends near Hassop.

13. Dennis the Deer

(Chatsworth – 20th century)

An animal tale with the human touch.

Dennis the deer looked glumly down at his reflection in the water and thought how miserable he appeared. Touching the water with his hoof, he noticed how quickly the ripples took away the sorry picture before him. Although this made him smile as he watched the ripples settle back into their mirror-like image, he was suddenly taken aback to see a strange face grinning up at him.

Not realising the intruder was of course the very same reflection which had previously looked so sad and forlorn, Dennis first looked one way and then looked the other and not seeing another deer in sight, he dropped his head between his legs to observe the scene behind him. Not a soul was to be seen. Dennis once again smiled to himself for being so silly as to think that anyone could possibly sneak up on him without his noticing, but his smile quickly turned into a snarl as he once again saw the smiling face at the waters edge.

Taking one step back and then with an almighty leap he pounced upon the creature before him and landed with a resounding splash into the water, almost covering himself from head to hoof.

Slowly making his way back to the embankment and shaking himself dry, it was then that he saw his reflection, preening himself in that watery looking glass. This time his smile was one of foolishness but also one which broadened to such an extent, that he could hardly quite believe that the handsome looking deer standing opposite was actually himself.

For most of his young life Dennis had been bad tempered, snapping at the heels of all the other deers his age and making a nuisance of himself into the bargain. That was until one day when finding himself all alone he began to wonder why none of the other deer would ever play with him. Always would he be the one left out when the others went on their little trips, leaving him with seemingly endless days without anyone to talk to.

Just as he was about to stalk away, head now bowed with his tail between his legs, there suddenly appeared by his side in the reflection of the water, the beautiful Debbie deer.

Turning his head to one side with Debbie doing likewise, their cold wet noses gently brushed against each other. Dennis immediately began to blush.

Quickly correcting himself and raising his body to its full height he then let out a manly snarl, but to his surprise, Debbie took no notice. For a second time he let out a ferocious snarl which was twice as loud as the last and which was also not very loud at all. Once more Debbie stood her ground and simply shook her head as if to say that it did not suit him one bit.

Looking at her with a puzzled expression on his face and holding his head to one side, Debbie then stared back into the water. Dennis not quite understanding, followed her direction only to see her beautiful smiling face at the side of his own very bad tempered one.

Stirring the water with her tiny hoof, Debbie then made the most nasty looking face she could. Then, allowing the ripples to settle once again, showed Dennis how she had looked beforehand.

Dennis dropped his head in embarrassment at the way he had treated her. Debbie again looked across at him and then down at the water, but this time she smiled her best smile of all as she stooped down and disturbed his reflection in the water with her nose. This time what Dennis saw appearing before him was the faintest glimmer of a smile upon his face, which, after a little prompting from Debbie, increased into a most huge and wondrous happy smile.

Having gained Dennis' confidence Debbie then pranced away, stopping and starting and inviting Dennis to do likewise. Needless to say it wasn't long before Dennis had joined her, jumping and frolicking in the summer sun and running away together in the direction of the old hunting tower on the hill.

Dennis had never before enjoyed himself so much in his young life, nor had he known such happiness and vowed forever to always have a smile upon his face no matter how sad he felt in the future.

THE MORAL OF THIS TALE
Try to see yourself as others do

DIRECTIONS AND HISTORY FILE

Chatsworth Park, which is a part of the Duke of Devonshire's large estate, may be approached from three different points. Journeying by car from Matlock or Bakewell on the A6 and travelling through Rowsley and Beeley on the B6012, the entrance to the park will lead directly to Chatsworth House where there are ample car parking facilities. An alternative route would be to travel to Edensor by way of the B6012 from Baslow or the A619 from Bakewell. Chatsworth may also be reached if parking at Nether End in Baslow, by crossing the little bridge over the stream and turning right to pass through the kissing gate and into the park itself.

Among the many interesting features in the park, which includes a childrens farmyard, the Deer are perhaps the most rewarding sight of all. Roaming freely around this beautifully landscaped enclosure, their timidity strongly resembles that which 'Dennis' portrayed, keeping well out of harms reach and communicating only among themselves.

Dennis the Deer gazing at his reflection in the river at Chatsworth.

14. Tip the Dog

(Howden Moor – 1954)

> An amazing feat of faithfulness from a dog towards his master.

Joseph Tagg and his dog 'Tip' spent many a happy hour walking along the banks of the reservoirs in Derwent Dale.

The eight mile stretch of these three reservoirs offered fond memories for Joseph and 'Tip'. Ladybower, with its lost villages which were flooded to make way for this great expanse of water, was where during the dry season once could be seen a church spire sticking out. Each year visitors from all over the world come to this panoramic scene of such tranquil beauty.

Joseph also remembered the war years when the Dambuster bombers did practise runs on the Derwent reservoir, whilst 'Tip' remembered and knew just where to find his favourite smells and sticks.

Late one December, Joseph decided to climb up onto Howden moor, and with a clear blue sky he knew that the view down the valley would be well worth the effort.

Letting his friends know of his intentions and where he would be walking – which is what all walkers in these parts do in case they become lost and fail to return on time – Joseph and 'Tip' set off on their walk.

With not a cloud in sight, Master and dog climbed steadily to the summit of the moor, stopping every once in a while to take in the magnificent views behind them.

When walking these hills it is quite easy to lose all track of time, so wild and alluring are their surroundings that it makes one feel you could walk forever. On a clear day this presents no problem but as often happens in the High Peak, unseen mists quickly sweep in from nowhere and before the unsuspecting walkers realise they are shrouded in thick fog – and the once clear day becomes a nightmare.

Down in the valley where Joseph and 'Tip' had so happily set off together on their journey, their friends were becoming increasingly worried. They had noticed the dark clouds rolling in from the west and that meant rain would surely follow, or worse still snowstorms.

The memorial at Howden Reservoir to Tip, the faithful sheepdog.

With no sight of the two travellers, a mountain rescue party was immediately organised in the hope of meeting Joseph and his dog on their return journey. However their search was to be curtailed. The higher they went the more severe the weather became, abandoning their cause with plans to try to locate them the following day.

As each day brought about more hazardous weather, the rescue party had no option but to wait until better conditions would afford them access onto the moor. The only hope they had was that man and dog may have found a hillside retreat where they could shelter for a few days until it was safe enough for them to attempt their journey home.

For fifteen weeks Joseph and 'Tip' remained on the high moors and it was not until the arrival of spring that a party of rescuers eventually found them.

Although 'Tip' survived, poor Joseph had not been able to last out the long winter months and had died due to the harsh conditions. The rescuers were quick to point out that 'Tip' was found still snuggling up to his master as if trying to keep him warm.

Such faithfulness was beyond anything the villagers could remember, and the story soon circulated about the faithful 'Tip'. Such was the amazing feat of this dog that a memorial stone was erected in his honour nearby the 'Dambusters' very own commemorative plaque.

THE MORAL OF THIS TALE
A friend in need is a friend indeed.

DIRECTIONS AND HISTORY FILE

The beginning of Derwent Dale forks off the A57 Snake Pass at Ladybower reservoir and continues up this valley to Fairholmes where the Derwent reservoir begins. It is by the side of this reservoir that you will notice the memorial stone to 'Tip' which is appropriately inscribed.

Further along this side road is the third reservoir of Howden leading up onto Howden Moor, where it is well advised to take extreme caution regardless what the weather. Advice and information may be secured at Fairholmes where there is also a mountain rescue post.

15. Harry the Hedgehog

(Peak National Park – 20th century)

> The hedgehog who had never heard about Christmas

Awakening after his long winters sleep, Harry the Hedgehog stretched his little legs and then, rubbing his eyes in the bright Spring sunshine, slowly made his way down to the river to quench his thirst.

"What a wonderful life I live," he thought to himself. "I can sleep all day and all night long through those horrible cold winter months, and then awaken to the springtime with all the new berries and green shoots just waiting for me to chew at to my hearts content." "Oh how lucky I am," he mused.

A few feet away from Harry stood two intelligent looking stags discussing the weather.

"Quite nice for this time of the year, George," said Rodney, the first stag.

"Very pleasant indeed Rodney, very pleasant indeed, although I must say I did enjoy this years snow. It made for some very entertaining fun don't you think?"

"Snow?", queried Harry looking up at the two graceful stags. "What is snow?" he asked them.

The stags looked down at Harry as if he wasn't there. "Snow . . ." said George rather snootily, " . . . is snow."

"Oh," said Harry, none the wiser.

"Snow, my dear and prickly friend, is frozen rain," snorted Rodney.

"Frozen rain? Brrr, I don't think I would much care for that," as Harry wrapped his arms around his body and shivered at the thought of it.

"Do you really mean to say that you have never seen snow?", sneered George.

"No, never," answered Harry, seemingly disinterested in the subject.

"Rodney, did you hear that? Imagine never having had a snowball fight."

"Nor ever having been sledging," added Rodney. "Where HAVE you been Hedgehog?"

"Missing all the fun and games," chipped in George.

"I, I've been asleep," Harry replied guiltily.

"Asleep, asleep? All winter?" Rodney's booming voice bellowed out.

"Why, yes. All hedgehogs go to sleep through the winter you know," Harry said meekly.

"Whatever for?" demanded George.

"Whatever for? Oh dear I don't really know, they just do, that's all," retorted Harry, who was by now getting quite fed up with all their silly questions.

"Father Christmas, Rodney?" implied George.

"Father Christmas, George," answered Rodney with an air of supreme knowledge.

Harry rubbed his eyes and blinked up at the two stags towering above him. "Father Christmas? Who is Father Christmas?" he asked.

Had the two stags not belonged to that select and chosen breed of animal selected to pull the sleigh of Father Christmas, they would undoubtedly have fallen about laughing, however they painstakingly explained to Harry just what he had been missing.

Listening intently to every word, Harry soon began to realise his great loss for not having celebrated Christmas and with his eyes now wide open, he eagerly questioned each attraction in turn.

"Stocking? Christmas tree? Sweets and nuts? Carols? Puddings and presents?" came Harry's started reply.

"All those and many more lovely surprises, all happening whilst you have been fast asleep," scolded Rodney.

"You should be ashamed of yourself hedgehog," scoffed George.

Harry blinked once more, hung his head and shuffled off in silence.

"Christmas . . . ," he could just be heard to say to himself, " . . . I will have to remember that, it sounds like waiting up for."

THE MORAL OF THIS TALE
Don't sleep your life away.

DIRECTIONS AND HISTORY FILE

As hedgehogs usually spend half their lives asleep whilst hibernating through the cold winter months, it is hardly surprising that one direction they take upon awakening is to seek out and replenish their food stores. Their journeys inevitably take them across some of our busy country roads below which run special 'Hedgehog Tunnels' allowing them to cross in perfect safety.

Two stags tell Harry the hedgehog about Christmas.

A shoal of freshwater trout.

16. The Young Trout

(River Derwent – 20th century)

> An unusual conversation between an angler and his catch.

Not so long ago, there was an angler who had a very frightening experience while standing on the banks of the river Derwent, fly fishing for trout.

Not having caught anything all morning, the fisherman decided at length to sit upon his basket and take his lunch, but it was just at that precise moment, there came a definite tug on his line.

Scrambling back to his feet and again taking a hold of his rod, he slowly began to reel his line in while at the same time being very careful not to lose whatever it was he had caught.

Reaching for his landing net in order to secure his catch and gently lowering it beneath the water's edge, he then with a sweep of his arm swiftly scooped up and out of the water what appeared to be a very young trout. Deftly taking the fish off the hook and inspecting the result of a dismal mornings fishing, he was amazed when the trout pitifully beseeched him.

"Please don't kill me mister, I'm only a young trout as you can see and there are so many things that I would like to see and do before I die."

The fisherman, who had no intention of killing such a young fish, was completely at a loss for words.

"You, you can talk!", was all he could manage to say.

"Of course I can talk, you can talk can't you?" replied the trout.

"But, but you're a fish," stammered his captor.

"That's right and my name is Tommy," said the fish rather indignantly.

Recovering from the shock of having a talking fish confronting him, the fisherman nevertheless considered himself fortunate to having caught something, talking fish or otherwise.

"Well Tommy," he said after awhile, "I must say that you are a clever little fish indeed, being able to talk the way you do."

By this time Tommy was getting rather dry with being out of the water for so long, and soon began to lie quite motionless in the fisherman's hands.

"I do hope you are not going to eat me," Tommy cried weakly.

The fisherman realising Tommy's concern, gently placed the little fish back into the water.

"There," said the fisherman kindly, "Now you can swim to your hearts content."

Flapping his tail in the shallow water, Tommy soon began to regain his strength and before long was splashing about as if he had never been on dry land at all. As the fisherman watched his every move, Tommy then gave one enormous jump as if to say thank you, waved goodbye and disappeared downstream.

It was some time before the fisherman could put the thought of the astonishing encounter to the back of his mind; and when eventually he did, he was to then believe that it had all been in his imagination.

As the months rolled by and each season came and went, the fisherman still fished his favourite spot without any further hindrance, not that was until early one Sunday morning when an almighty tug on his line almost caused him to fall flat on his face in the river.

Quickly taking a firmer grip on his rod and reeling in the tension, it was then that he realised that he must have caught his line in the reeds, either that or he had caught a very large fish indeed.

So strong was the pull on his line that he decided to allow it to find its own direction.

Steadily but surely the line began to float down to where he was standing, just as if it was being guided by some unknown force. Believing his line now to be free, he slowly wound it in, until there, lying down at his feet and quite still except for the graceful swishing of its tail, was the biggest and most beautiful trout he had ever seen. Cradling the trout in his arms and placing it on the bank, he could not but help notice the sad pleading eyes staring up at him.

"It couldn't be," he muttered to himself. Looking around to make sure he wasn't being watched, the fisherman then spoke in a very soft voice.

"Tommy? Tommy is that you?" No reply.

Pouring a little water over the motionless body, the fish immediately began to respond, blinking and opening his mouth and at the same time, issuing a faint whisper.

"You remembered me," he spluttered.

"Tommy, I don't believe it," the fisherman joyfully cried picking up the large trout and settling him back in the water. "What a lovely surprise, I hope you haven't hurt yourself."

"Just getting my breath" panted Tommy.

"Why, it must be almost three years since I last saw you, and look at you, how you've grown."

Tommy gradually started showing signs of his old self again, first splashing one way and then the other until finally coming to rest at the feet of the fisherman.

"There, now I feel much better. At first I thought I had got tangled up in somebody's broken line. You would be surprised how many dangers there are in the river for us fishes: broken lines, broken bottles, rusty cans, bits of barbed wire, why, it's a wonder there are any of us left alive, not to mention those horrible fishermen who don't throw us back," said Tommy.

The fisherman looked sympathetically at Tommy, well aware of some of the cruel methods used by other anglers. Although he himself had always been a very keen angler, he did nevertheless always throw his catch back into the river and did at times consider it to be a rather cruel sport.

Taking out a sandwich from his basket and breaking it up, he then sprinkled a few tiny pieces down to where his friend lay, who in turn took them as if he hadn't eaten in weeks.

"Now, Tommy, tell me what you've been doing with yourself since we last met?", the fisherman asked good naturedly.

"Well," replied Tommy between a mouthful of bread and tomato, "when I left you I was so fed up with just swimming around in the same old river, that I decided to travel around the world and see if all the stories I had heard were really true."

"And were they?" enquired the kindly fisherman.

"Oh yes, there were some lovely sights to see, especially the other fishes with all their strange shapes and beautiful colours. But the more I travelled the more I realised that everything that I really wanted was right back here in my own river."

Tommy paused to take in further refreshment and thought how nice it was to be able to eat some proper food, instead of all those foreign concoctions.

"You see," he went on continuing with his story, "the rivers are the same, the trees are the same and the sun and the moon still show day and night, in fact just about everything is exactly the same. Everything that is except for my friends which I missed very much." The fisherman smiled down at Tommy, knowing well how true his story was.

"Will you be going away again then Tommy?" he asked lightheartedly. "Only if I can take my friends with me," chortled Tommy. Then with a swish of his tail and a fond farewell to his friend, he hurriedly made his way upstream to join his chums.

THE MORAL OF THIS TALE

The grass is not necessarily greener on the other side of the hill.

DIRECTIONS AND HISTORY FILE

The source of the River Derwent springs from the Bleaklow stones high up on Bleaklow Moor. Coursing through the Ladybower reservoir it then joins with the rivers Noe and the Wye before linking with the river Trent to eventually flow out into the open sea.

Tommy the trout.

17. The Little Yellow Rabbit

(Peak National Park – 20th century)

Thinking he was actually yellow in colour, the little rabbit is in for a big surprise.

Out of all the hundreds of rabbits who were jumping and frolicking about in the lush green meadow, there was one who stood out more than any of the others.

Not that he had two heads or anything silly like that, nor two bushy tails. You see whereas all the other rabbits were brown, black or white, he was in actual fact coloured yellow, and it was because of this that none of the other rabbits wanted to play with him. In fact they would rather poke fun at him because of his unusual colour. Some went as far as saying that he was yellow in colour because he was a scaredy-cat. This got the little yellow rabbit into all kinds of trouble, especially in the school playground.

Sitting all alone as he watched the others having such a great time with their fun and games, he slowly became more and more downcast and wondered why there were no other yellow rabbits like himself. Wiping a tear away he was suddenly joined by a large brown owl who had swooped down to sit beside him.

At first this frightened the little rabbit who knew how dangerous these birds of prey could be.

"It's all right," said the brown owl, "I'm not going to eat you, after all . . .," he laughed, "who would want to eat a yellow rabbit?"

More tears ran down the little rabbit's cheeks and seeing how upset he was, the owl wrapped his wing around him and whispered to him soothingly.

"I once knew your mother you know," he comforted.

"You did?" questioned the rabbit in surprise.

"Oh yes, and your father too. We used to share the same field together. Mind you that was when there was plenty of food for everyone until the townspeople came and spoiled everything."

The little rabbit looked up at the wise old owl and wondered what was the reasoning behind his confessions and friendliness. The old owl began to explain.

"Once there were no roads at all in this area, only tracks where all the animals were safe to go about their business. Unfortunately as the years progressed and the human population increased, more and more land was taken away from the countryside and used for building houses, and as you know, where there are houses there are roads, and where there are roads, there are motor vehicles carrying the humans back and forth to wherever they have to go." "Well . . . ," continued the owl pushing his spectacles higher up his nose, "As your mummy would have explained had she been alive today, one day your father ventured off to work in the big city. Being a country rabbit he was quite unaware of what dangers lay in those places, and, after he met with a fatal accident, your mummy decided that the same fate should not happen to you."

The little yellow rabbit still could not understand why the old owl was telling him all this, some of which he already knew.

"It was then," went on the owl, "that your mummy knitted you a brightly coloured yellow jumper when you were only a little boy. She placed it over your head and covered your whole body and then zipped it from top to bottom so that you would be noticed whenever straying out onto the open road. That was just before she died," concluded the owl.

The wise old owl, after telling the story, pointed to the jumper the little yellow rabbit was still wearing. Fumbling beneath the collar he slowly unzipped the jumper so as not to catch the rabbit's fur in the zip, and to everyones amazement, out flopped the most beautiful . . . . no not a rabbit, but a handsome white hare who at once became the envy of all for miles around.

THE MORAL OF THIS TALE
Better to be safe than sorry.

DIRECTIONS AND HISTORY FILE

The only directions relating to this story, are those which relate to the Highway Code. Where children are concerned it is always advisable to wear some form of fluorescent clothing, and at night, always wear something light coloured.

18. Gilbert the Grouse

(Edale –1995)

A cheeky grouse known affectionately as Gilbert becomes a nuisance to villagers and ramblers.

Lurking around the foothills which lead to the Pennine Way through the village of Edale, there was a most disgruntled and angry bird called Gilbert.

Widely known to the many walkers who take to these hills, Gilbert is in actual fact a moorland bird about the size of a football and being a grouse is classified as a game-bird and is constantly being hunted by shooting parties and poachers.

So timid and wary are these birds, that at the slightest sound they will suddenly appear out of the heather making the most awful and undignified racket imaginable, then retreat out of harms way screeching their familiar warning cry of 'Go-back, Go-back'. Gilbert however would have none of this.

Instead of taking flight with his other grouse friends, he would immediately seize upon the opportunity to attack anybody who came near to him and proceed to scare them half to death.

Perhaps the name 'grouse' was quite appropriate for Gilbert, perhaps also he had been the 'black sheep' in his family, an expression used when one member decides to go his or her own way regardless of their parents advice, believing that they know better. This of course often leads them into all kinds of trouble.

No-one really knows what made Gilbert as nasty and as unpredictable as he was, only the trouble he caused.

So it was that when Gilbert grew into adulthood, he remained alone and unwanted by the other grouse because of his foolhardiness and for the pickles he would get into.

One of his many pranks would be to lie in wait among the heather then suddenly fly out at unsuspecting passers-by chasing them well off their chosen routes. Similarly, upon seeing an unattended haversack, he would boldly seek it out to stand guard over it letting no-one near, much to the frustration of the owner.

With residents and walkers alike in Edale, Gilbert showed no mercy. Children would scatter at his presence, parents would wave their arms and ramblers their sticks, and everyone in general would take cover as he dived and flew over them, all the time screeching and squawking in a most threatening manner.

When at last he tired of his troublesome antics, the wayward bird would scuttle back into the heather to restore his energy for the following day, when once more would he start all over again.

As the long hot summer months gradually gave way to winters blustery showers, so did the sightings of Gilbert. Whether he had changed his ways or whether he just didn't like the cold remains to be seen. No matter what the reason, when wandering through this pleasant village you would be well advised to keep a sharp look-out, for Gilbert may well decide to fly true to form again turning your quiet stroll into an all out jog!

THE MORAL OF THIS TALE
There was a serpent even in the garden of Eden.

DIRECTIONS AND HISTORY FILE

Turning right off the A625 in Hope travel between the two steep slopes of Win Hill and Lose Hill, where the vale of Edale leads directly to the picturesque village of the same name.
Gilbert the grouse, as he was affectionately known, probably by those who had not been attacked by him, might well have been disturbed by the extraordinarily hot weather of this particular year. There have been many other strange cases affecting animals in the Peak District which have also been put down to the weather. Perhaps another year will give us a clearer picture.

Gilbert the grouse.

19. The Cow Jumped Over the Cliff

(Ashford-Bakewell –1907)

> The story of a cow who fell 50 feet down a cliff
> and lived to tell the tale.

As we all know in the famous nursery rhyme, 'the cow jumped over the moon', but did you know that here in the Peak District there was another cow who almost equalled those dizzy heights?

Upon being driven from Ashford to Bakewell market one Monday morning, sniffing the air as she lumbered along the narrow lanes, Sally the cow, as she was affectionately known, suddenly came to an abrupt halt. Whether it was the scent of the nearing market which caused her to disobey the orders of her handlers, no-one knows.

Sally had heard many a tale about the cattle market in Bakewell. Some of her friends who had returned from that place told about how, upon their arrival, they had been packed into little pens like sardines, had labels pasted upon their backs and were constantly being tapped on the nose and prodded in the ribs with long bamboo poles. There were her other friends whom she never saw again, and Sally often wondered what had become of them.

Sniffing at the cold morning air again, and receiving yet another smack on her behind for being so disobedient, Sally at last made up her mind.

Not wishing to suffer such indignities, she bellowed out her defiance for the very last time, turned, and headed straight for the woods, leaving her handlers following in her wake.

Careering through the undergrowth and dodging each tree as she came to them, Sally smiled at the thought of having outsmarted her would-be aggressors. Thoroughly enjoying herself as first she swayed one way and then the other, it was not until reaching a clearing in the woods that she was to notice, all too late, the fast approaching edge of the cliff top which fell some fifty feet below.

Unable to slow down in time due to her heavy bulk and the speed with which she was travelling, Sally instinctively tried to jump to safety, only to find herself hurtling down the cliff face towards the road below and to what seemed like certain death.

When her handlers reached the point from which Sally had fallen, they were to witness a most amazing piece of good fortune for the animal. During her fall, Sally first of all encountered a tree growing out of the cliff face. Meeting it with all her weight and uprooting the large plant, she was relieved to find herself not falling as fast as when she first left the top of the cliff.

Her second encounter was even more welcome than the last.

As she gradually picked up speed again, Sally suddenly found herself straddled across a series of telephone wires, from which she dropped somewhat unceremoniously onto the road. Without the tree and the telephone wires to break her fall, she knew she would have surely died.

Looking back up the cliff face, Sally could just see her handlers peering over the top. Smiling to herself once again, she gently rolled over, got to her feet and quietly walked off as if nothing had happened, finally breaking into a jog to find pastures new.

THE MORAL OF THIS TALE
Look before you leap.

DIRECTIONS AND HISTORY FILE

Bakewell, which is also known as the 'Capital of the Peak', has long been famous for its Monday market. Central to the Peak District on the A6, Bakewell is therefore ideally situated to accommodate the out-lying farms which rely heavily upon its cattle market for selling their produce. A second market caters more for the domestic side of life, attracting visitors from all walks of life.

Sally the cow after her amazing jump!

20. Dragons and Flying Saucers

(Peak National Park – 17th - 20th century)

A collection of strange sightings including dragons, giant dogs, panthers, wallabies and U.F.O's.

In the days when knights rode their chargers along the highways and byways of the Peak District, fearlessly meeting any challenge laid down before them, there was of course no challenger more worthy of testing their skills than that old adversary the legendary dragon. Had these dragons played fair and remained on the ground, the knights would have had little or no trouble in ridding the land of them once and for all. Unfortunately however, the dragon was still being reported circling the skies long after those noble knights ceased to combat with horse and lance.

As far back as the seventeenth century, before science fiction became known, fiery dragons were seen to fly over the peaceful countryside, nostrils flaring and belching out flames of fire, terrorising not only livestock, but whole communities.

Accompanying these flying beasts were also a variety of serpents with their probing eyes of assorted colours, endlessly searching the ground below as if seeking their next meal.

All through the ages there have always been mysterious lights appearing in the sky. By today's standards, these lights are now classified as U.F.O's or unidentified flying objects, which are usually associated with beings from other planets.

Most accounts which cannot normally be explained are usually handed down by word of mouth, one person passing on the information to another, thus being blown out of all proportion after having been related several times over from its original description.

Superstition always seemed to play its part in magnifying what was in the first instance merely guess work at explaining the unexplained. The most common of all these reports of these strange creatures are the big black dogs said to roam this beautiful countryside. Unattended and wild in origin, these animals were first known as 'Boggarts', a ghostly dog belonging to the spirit world and considered to bring bad luck to anyone catching sight of them.

Such was their frightening reputation, that well before the hour of darkness the villagers would lock and bolt their doors and windows, never to step outside until first light the following day.

Although pet lovers have been known to keep such ferocious animals as Panthers, Pumas, Lynx and Bobcats, never has there really been any definite proof that they were actually roaming freely around the Peak. The remains of carcases belonging to sheep and cattle have on occasions been attributed to these animals, accompanied at times with photographic evidence, but so obscure have these photographs been that the mystery still remains to this day.

One strange animal that really was seen leaping around the Peak District was the Wallaby. Twelve thousand miles from their original habitat in Australia, these Kangaroo-like marsupials were thought to have escaped the compounds where they were being held during the second world war. Finding freedom in the local countryside, it was decided to leave them to their own devices, whereupon they probably died out due to the harsh winters for which this area is noted.

Other strange sightings recorded include Mermaids swimming in the reservoirs on Kinder Scout *(see page 20)* and at Buxton, luring people down into their murky depths with the promise of everlasting life.

Hobs, Goblins and Fairies *(see page 25)* are still frequently seen by the superstitious, and are often treated with the greatest respect if stumbled across.

White ladies in long flowing gowns *(see page 40)* are among the many ghostly apparitions connected with the old halls and manors of the Peak District, some seeming content to walk around their old haunts, whilst others try to re-live their past lives causing distress for those who have taken their places.

Looking back at all these strange creatures which appear to have made their home in the Peak District, it is astonishing that although we are able to put men on the moon, we can at the same time associate ourselves with such fantastic tales.

Perhaps when all is said and done, the fiery dragons or U.F.O's as they are now known, will swoop down from the sky to capture and domesticate the big black dogs, round up the odd Wallaby for use as a cuddly toy, catch the mermaids and place them in a 'mermaid bowl', far better than goldfish, after which the fairies could amuse themselves by sitting on the brim with their little fishing rods!

Finally, the occupants of the U.F.O's could marry the white ladies, thus returning back to their planet to all live happily ever after!

THE MORAL OF THIS TALE
Seeing is believing.

DIRECTIONS AND HISTORY FILE

The Peak District National Park is set in the wilds of North West Derbyshire. First opened in 1951, it is the world's second largest park covering an area of some eighty square miles of open access country along with 1600 miles of footpaths.

Attracting twenty two million visitors each year from all over the world, 'The Peak' is a natural source of untouched beauty and great historical interest.

Dragons, fairies, flying saucers and a fairytale castle.